SCHUMANN

PIANO CONCERTO IN A MINOR   OPUS 54

for Piano Solo and Orchestra (Arranged for Second Piano)

EDITED BY THOMAS LABÉ

AN ALFRED MASTERWORK EDITION

Cover art: The Marketplace at Zwickau, *1833*
Johann Gottfried Pulian (1809–1875)
Oil on canvas
Städtische Museen Zwickau, Art collection
Inv. no. V/79/18/K1

The tall building with the tower (right) is the Zwickau Gewandhaus where the Piano Concerto in A Minor was performed on July 10, 1847 with Clara Schumann as soloist.

ROBERT SCHUMANN
Piano Concerto in A Minor, Op. 54
for Piano Solo and Orchestra (Arranged for Second Piano)

Edited by Thomas Labé

Contents

Foreword

When the autograph manuscript of Schumann's sole piano concerto came up for sale in the fall of 1989, it was described in Sotheby's catalog as "the most important manuscript of Robert Schumann to have been offered for sale at auction this century."[1] Sold on November 23 to a dealer representing a consortium of German public and private donors, the extraordinary sum brought by the manuscript (nearly $1.4 million) was a measure not only of its worth, but of the special position the work enjoys among music lovers the world over. It is now housed in the archive of the Heinrich-Heine-Institut, Düsseldorf,[2] where it is accessible to scholars and performers alike. Prior to the sale, the manuscript formed part of the private, extensive collection of Schumanniana amassed by Alfred Wiede (1864–1929) who had purchased it in May 1912 from the eldest Schumann daughter Marie (1841–1929).

Lithograph of Robert and Clara Schumann by Eduard Kaiser (Vienna, 1847)

Conceived in two separate bursts of creative activity over four years apart, details of the concerto's intermittent process of composition were entered in pencil by the composer on the lower left hand corner of the manuscript's fly leaf: "Allegro Leipzig 1841/Intermezzo and Rondo Dresden 1845." The work was premiered in Dresden on December 4, 1845 with Ferdinand Hiller (1811–1885), the work's dedicatee, conducting and Clara Schumann (1819–1896), the composer's wife, as soloist. It has since gained a place among the composer's most beloved and often-heard works and, indeed, stands as a cornerstone of the concerto repertoire.

Acknowledgments

Producing a new edition of the Schumann Piano Concerto in A Minor has been truly a labor of love. It would not have been possible without the generous assistance of a number of individuals and institutions. I wish to thank Marianne Tilch and the staff of the Heinrich-Heine-Institut, Düsseldorf, for allowing me to examine the autograph manuscript; Gerd Nauhaus and the staff of the Robert-Schumann-Haus, for providing valuable information and access to a host of materials during my visit to Zwickau; Stefanie Johnson, for her expert advice concerning translations from the original German; E. L. Lancaster, Vice President, Keyboard Editor-in-Chief of Alfred Publishing, for involving me in the project, and Sharon Aaronson, Senior Masterwork Editor, for her invaluable criticisms and equally valuable suggestions and encouragement through all the stages of publication; and my wife Hyunsoon and daughter Courtney, for their endless patience and support.

The Diaries and Household Books

For Schumann, like so many of his Romantic generation counterparts, the diary was the quintessential form of artistic expression. Far more than a record of daily events, it was a repository for literary and philosophical musings, dreams and visions, and innermost thoughts (quite often expressed in affectionate terms). Robert and Clara began a joint "marriage diary" the day after their September 12, 1840 wedding, and kept it for several years. The household books, comprised primarily of detailed records of income and expenditures, served as miniature diaries for Schumann's middle period as well. They also performed a useful function in helping Schumann counter the charges of irresponsibility leveled by Clara's father, who sought to block their wedding plans.

Schumann and the Piano Concerto

At the age of 17, Robert Schumann (1810–1856) began keeping copious diaries, a practice he would maintain for nearly the rest of his life. From these it is evident that he felt an early attraction to the genre of the piano concerto. In 1827, among other compositional efforts, he "began a piano concerto in E minor."[3] In December of the following year, he made note in the diary of two consecutive evenings spent "composing a [piano] concerto in E-flat major."[4] And although not specifically mentioned by Schumann, his early sketchbooks also contain fragments of at least two other projected concerti.[5] None of these were brought to completion.

In 1830, having finally abandoned his law studies in favor of music, Schumann settled in Leipzig. With his sights set on a concert career, he began a formal course of study with the renowned teacher Friedrich Wieck (1785–1873), who pledged to "make Robert into one of the greatest living pianists."[6] To realize success in such an endeavor, Schumann knew well he would have to meet the public expectation of original, virtuoso works. The project book ascribes the origins of three compositions to the year, all no doubt conceived to that end:

> Began a piano concerto in F major
>
> Variations on the name Abegg (my first published opus —only half the variations are printed)
>
> Toccata[7]

Most ambitious among these was the large, virtuoso concerto. Schumann completed the work's first movement in the summer of 1831, and gave its solo part a private hearing on August 14.[8] Scattered over some 35 pages of a sketchbook,[9] the elaborate passagework betrays a work fashioned after that of the reigning Parisian virtuosi—Henri Herz (1803–1888), Franz Hünten (1793–1878), Johann Nepomuk Hummel (1778–1837), Friedrich [Wilhelm Michael] Kalkbrenner (1785–1849), et al. In their hands, concerted works (many of which Schumann had either studied, performed, or were to be found in his music collection at the time[10]) were little more than a convenient platform from which to display a performer's ability. With the orchestra relegated to a near inconsequential role (contributing scarcely more than light accompaniment and the occasional requisite tutti interjection), such works made no pretext towards serious composition.[11] Although Schumann would later come to reject this style altogether, he thought highly enough of the effort to forward its opening solo for appraisal to the pianist and composer Hummel,[12] to whom he also apparently intended to dedicate the work.[13]

Schumann's performing ambitions, however, were destined to remain unfulfilled. His erratic practice habits, experimentation with mechanical devices (imagined to improve finger strength), and generally dissolute lifestyle, contributed to a total laming of his right hand by October 1831. Despite a number of treatments (including the notorious folk remedy of "animal baths"), he wrote to his mother in November 1832 that "so far as my hand is concerned, the doctor is always consoling; I, for my part, am fully resigned and regard it as incurable."[14] Unable to further pursue his career plan, and having no longer the need for large scale, virtuoso vehicles for piano and orchestra, he subsequently abandoned not only the F major concerto but also his original concept of the *Abegg* Variations (Op. 1) as a work for piano and orchestra. All that survives of a planned orchestral accompaniment to the set is an introduction, notated in short score, found in an early sketchbook.[15]

Although Schumann would not set out to compose another piano concerto until the end of the decade, his activities in the intervening period provide ample evidence that the genre had not lost its appeal. Over the winter of 1833–34 he assisted Wieck's daughter Clara with the orchestration of her Piano Concerto in A Minor, Op. 7, an ambitious work, which her father had hoped would "attract the attention of the connoisseurs."[16] And with the publication of the first issue (on March 3, 1834) of the *Neue Leipziger Zeitschrift für Musik* (New Leipzig Journal of Music), Schumann had found not only a forum for written expression of his creative ideas, but the means by which he could examine and review a large number of musical works, not least of which would be piano concerti.

Lithograph of Clara Wieck by E. C. Fechner (Paris, 1832)

Robert-Schumann-Haus Zwickau; Archiv-Nr.: 10562–B2

Schumann's first review, published in 1831, had in fact been of a work for piano and orchestra, the Variations on *Lá ci darem la mano*, Op. 2 of Frédéric Chopin (1810–1849). Writing in Leipzig's *Allgemeine Musikalische Zeitung*, he hardly seemed troubled by the favoritism shown the piano over the orchestra (the latter, he observed, played only the role of a "small cohort"[17]). However, by 1836, having assumed full managerial and editorial responsibilities for the *Neue Zeitschrift*, Schumann's viewpoint changed considerably. He berated contemporary composers for conceiving the solo sections of concerti before the orchestral tuttis, and declared such emphasis placed on the solo instrument near unconstitutional.[18]

Indeed, a good portion of Schumann's reviews are given over to consideration of the balance between piano and orchestra. Schumann recognized the ability of the newer pianos of his day to create a comprehensive, almost orchestral effect, and the challenge this posed to the traditional exchange between solo instrument and orchestra. And despite his considerably more circumspect view of the genre—the carefully balanced classical models had become a regular part of Leipzig musical life—he still wondered if the piano concerto was destined to become "obsolete."[19] Not until the arrival in Leipzig of Felix Mendelssohn (1809–1847), who assumed directorship of the Gewandhaus Orchestra in late 1835, did Schumann see a viable new direction for the genre. In addition to bringing before the public many works of Mozart and Beethoven that had not been heard there before,[20] Mendelssohn gave hearings of the newer, nonvirtuosic concerti by some Romantic composers who were going against the tide. Mendelssohn's performance of his own First Piano Concerto in G Minor, Op. 25, had made a deep impression on Schumann.[21] The same work even occasioned such a conservative critic as Berlin's Ludwig Rellstab (1799–1860) to complain of an orchestral dominance in the first movement.[22]

In the fall of 1838, Schumann journeyed to Vienna, seeking a new publisher for the *Neue Zeitschrift*. Although ultimately unsuccessful in this regard, his time spent in the Austrian capital was nevertheless productive. He composed and published there a number of solo piano works (Opp. 18, 19, 20, 23 and 26), and continued making contributions to the journal. Among the articles he sent back to Leipzig for publication was a review of the

The Neue Zeitschrift für Musik

Schumann was the guiding member among the founders of the New Leipzig Journal of Music "published by a society of artists and friends of art." Julius Knorr, the first editor-in-chief, was soon incapacitated by illness, and Schumann consequently assumed all editorial and managerial responsibilities. When the journal appeared in 1835 with "Leipzig" removed from the title, the masthead read "under the direction of Robert Schumann." In the ensuing years, Schumann wrote scores of articles and reviewed hundreds of musical works in the cause of the journal. From 1840, he considerably decreased his contributions, thereby allowing more time for composition, and relinquished the editorship altogether in 1844.

Clara Wieck

Born on September 13, 1819 to Friedrich Wieck and his first wife Marianne Tromlitz (1797–1872), she inherited a musical background. Her father was a noted teacher and music dealer in Leipzig, and her mother had performed frequently as a vocal and piano soloist at the Leipzig Gewandhaus. Under her father's care-ful, if somewhat overbearing, tutelage, Clara quickly developed into an accomplished pianist. Her first appear-ance at the Gewandhaus in 1828 was followed by a series of fortuitous tours arranged and accompanied by her father, all of which served to rapidly spread her fame. One of the foremost pianists of her generation, her concert career extended over 50 years, during which time she was the most frequently heard soloist at the Gewandhaus. The 50th anniversary of her debut there was celebrated in a special jubilee con-cert in 1878.

Concerto No. 7, Op. 93 ("Pathétique") by Ignaz Moscheles (1794–1870), and Mendelssohn's Second Concerto, Op. 40. Schumann commended both works for their avoidance of virtuosity, though he cautioned in the case of Mendelssohn's piece, that concerti should not be totally devoid of opportunity for brilliant display. He also took the occasion to offer a general assessment of the genre, for which he clearly had more in mind, concluding that "we must yet await the genius who will show us a brilliant new way of combining orchestra and piano."[23]

Not long after the article's publication Schumann aspired to this vision himself. "I am willing to consider a symphony," he wrote to his fiancée Clara Wieck on January 16, 1839, "but first I must finish the concerto."[24] This initial reference to a planned work in D minor was followed a few days later by news that "the first movement is finished … the orchestration is coming along very well," and that the concerto "is neither difficult to play nor to grasp."[25] On January 26 he wrote again to Clara, describing a work that "lies somewhere between a symphony, concerto and a large sonata; I see that I cannot write a concerto for the virtuosi; I have to think of something else."[26]

Indeed, what survives of the planned D minor concerto does exhibit a conscious effort to realize a piano concerto considerably distanced from what current practice pre-scribed. Eschewing any suggestion of bravura show, a sizeable portion of the musical emphasis is assigned to the orchestra, reducing the piano to an almost obligato pres-ence. A concern for formal innovation is also apparent in the movement's slow introduction (quite unusual for a concerto), along with the presence of four measures labeled "scherzo" (also in D minor), found in the manuscript.[27] One can only wonder what Schumann might have composed for on February 20 he made the discouraging observation "concerto still not finished,"[28] and subsequently abandoned the work. Nonetheless, the D minor concerto movement marked an important return to writ-ing for orchestral forces following a lengthy hiatus—his last significant effort had been the so-called *Zwickauer* Symphony (G minor) of 1832–33—and forged a link between compo-sition for the instrument with which he most closely associated, and his forthcoming symphonic efforts.

Schumann married Clara Wieck on September 12, 1840, putting behind him the lengthy, contentious dispute with her father. Not long thereafter, he expressed the desire, in their joint marriage diary, that Clara delay her touring plans so that he might first compose "a symphony and a piano concerto."[29] The concerto, he noted in the project book, would be "in a form all my own."[30] It is easy to see why Schumann was anxious to achieve success in the realm of orchestral composition. Within the relatively narrow confines of his activity, the symphony concerts (especially those at Leipzig's renowned Gewandhaus) constituted the principal musical forum. As Alfred Dörfell (1821–1905)—who would later compile the first catalog of Schumann's music—pointed out, for all the highly original solo piano works he had published, not to mention his voluminous writings for the *Neue Zeitschrift*, by 1840 Schumann had attained precious little in the way of public recognition.[31]

On March 31, 1841, Schumann's First Symphony ("Spring") in B-flat Major, Op. 38 was successfully premiered at the Leipzig Gewandhaus under Mendelssohn's baton. Anxious to reiterate his accomplishment, work on several other orchestral compositions followed in close order. Observed Clara in early May: "For three days he has been orchestrating his second large-scale orchestral work … it consists of an Overture, Scherzo and Finale [Op. 52], and has already a new idea for a piano fantasy with orchestra, one on which I really hope he will follow through."[32] The fantasy was drafted between May 4 and May 14,[33] with completion of the orchestration by May 22 confirmed in the marriage diary: "The *Symphonette* [Op. 52] is completely orchestrated, as is a fantasy for piano and orchestra. New ideas are rising within me, yet there is much to be done on what I've already written."[34]

Schumann might well have had the celebrated *Konzertstück*, J. 282 (1821) of Carl Maria von Weber (1786–1826) in mind when he penned the fantasy. In Weber's **work**, four varied sections are drawn together to form a single movement. Schumann had himself proposed a similar scheme in an 1836 review of Moscheles's Fifth and Sixth Concerti: "One imagines," he wrote, "a type of one-movement composition in moderate tempo in which an introductory or prefatory part would assume the place of a first allegro, a cantabile section that of an adagio, and a brilliant conclusion that of a rondo."[35] The fantasy, with its opening *Allegro*, ensuing *Andante espressivo*, and coda (*Allegro molto*) recalls precisely this formal outline. As Claudia Macdonald has pointed out, it was not Schumann's intention to simply elide the traditional three movements of concerto structure, but rather to bring out their various affects within the course of a single movement.[36]

Schumann wasted no time in seeking out a performance of the fantasy. On June 6 he wrote to Hippolyte André Chélard (1789–1861), Hofkapellmeister in Weimar: "I have completed a new instrumental piece—Overture, Intermezzo and Finale [Op. 52]—and a fantasy for piano and orchestra that I hope will be performed here next winter. Perhaps we could also try out the fantasy in Weimar. That would certainly be to my satisfaction."[37] In the meantime, circumstance would provide a more immediate opportunity to hear the fantasy in Leipzig.

At the instigation of Hermann Härtel (1803–1875) Schumann had approached the concertmaster and acting director of the Gewandhaus, Ferdinand David (1810–1874), with a proposal to try out his First Symphony in its revised form. From quite early on, Schumann had come to rely on such hearings of his symphonic works as a means to test the orchestration and used the results as a basis for modifications.[38] Schumann's awkward manner was humorously recounted by David: "After an hour, it became clear to me that he would like to hear his symphony in public once more. He then smoked two cigars, passed his hand over his mouth twice because a syllable wanted to come out, took his hat, forgot his gloves, nodded with his head, went to the wrong door, then the right one, then disappeared."[39] The necessary details were conveyed to Schumann in a letter from David (who would also conduct the rehearsal) dated August 12: "The only time for your rehearsal is tomorrow, Friday, at 10 o'clock … If you are satisfied with tomorrow morning, then tell the bearer of this [message], who will make all the arrangements immediately."[40]

The fantasy, now "refined and ready to be played,"[41] would also be heard. "Friday or Saturday a small rehearsal of my husband's symphony will be held before it is sent off to be printed, and I will play the fantasy with orchestra, to which I am very much looking forward. That is what has been decided today, and I wanted to inform you right away,"[42] wrote Clara to the Schumanns' friend Ernst Adolf Becker (1798–1874). Payment of one Thaler and twenty Neugroschen to an unidentified copyist for preparation of the performance parts was registered in the household book on August 12.[43]

Just two weeks before going into labor with their first child (Marie), Clara recorded her impression of the rehearsal in the marriage diary:

> *I played the fantasy in A minor as well. Unfortunately, it brought me very little enjoyment, on account of the hall being empty. I could hear neither myself, nor the orchestra. However, having played it twice, I discovered that when thoroughly rehearsed, it must certainly bring the most pleasurable experience to any listener. The piano is so tightly interwoven with the orchestra that you can't envision one without the other. I look forward to playing it in public, where certainly it must sound differently than in today's rehearsal. Robert nonetheless took delight in it. He could easily have heard it several more times, as could I have played it several more times.*[44]

Schumann voiced a similar reaction to Mendelssohn. Despite some shortcomings on the part of the orchestra, wrote Schumann, "it brought me great pleasure."[45]

Not long after the rehearsal, characteristic revisions to the score were reported by Clara in the marriage diary on August 20: "He has now refined his fantasy, here and there deleting

The Leipzig Gewandhaus

The Gewandhaus ("cloth-hall") as Schumann knew it was built in 1781, and newly refurbished during the summer of 1833. The high standards that had been established by the orchestra were heightened by Mendelssohn, who made the Gewandhaus ensemble into one of the finest in all of Germany. It was here that many of Schumann's works were premiered, including the first, second and fourth (early version) symphonies.

Schumann's illness

The exact nature of the recurring, severe depressive episodes, which plagued Schumann throughout his life (the first of which occurred in 1833, and was perhaps brought on by the deaths of his brother Julius and sister-in-law Rosalie in close succession), remains elusive. The traditionally held view that Schumann had contracted syphilis as a young man, while certainly plausible, falls short of providing a fully satisfying explanation for his symptoms. In a failed suicide attempt in 1854, Schumann threw himself into the Rhine river. During his subsequent incarceration at the asylum overseen by Dr. Richarz in Endenich, he was never able to regain his health. He died there of self starvation on July 29, 1856.

a horn or bassoon, and while I am writing this he works on his Overture, Scherzo and Finale, to soon finish that as well."[46] With the fantasy now complete, Schumann reserved an opus number for it [48][47] and set out to find a publisher. The task would be considerable, as few would venture to bring through the press any such work that had not yet found an audience. And although individual movements of three-movement concerti at times found their way onto concert programs, on such occasions it was most often to be the second, third, or both latter movements.[48] Schumann's initial inquiries to the publishers Friedrich Kistner in Leipzig (August 1841) and Julius Schuberth in Hamburg (November 1842) predictably did not meet with any success.

It may have been in connection with yet another appeal to a publisher (this time Friedrich Whistling in Leipzig[49]) that Schumann returned to the score of the fantasy in early 1843. On January 11 the household book reads "worked a lot on the fantasy," and "the same," for the following day. On January 13 is written "busy with the concerto piece."[50] Whether he actually revised the score, or was simply referring to his ongoing efforts to find the work a publisher is not clear. He may also have been reviewing the work on Clara's account as she was contemplating a performance, at the invitation of singer Sophie Schloß (1822–1903), in a special concert to be held at the Gewandhaus on February 9. "I don't know yet whether or not I will play the quintet or the concerto piece with orchestra by Robert. One of them it will be, that's for certain," she wrote to her father on January 23.[51] Clara opted in favor of the Piano Quintet (Op. 44).[52]

Schumann's further efforts to realize the work in print included discussions with Prague publisher Jan Hoffmann (who visited Schumann in May 1843) and correspondence with Carl Gotthelf Böhme (of the Leipzig publishing concern C. F. Peters[53]). Neither showed much interest. With all else having failed, in December 1843 he offered the work to Hermann Härtel without fee ("as a gesture of good will"[54]) on condition that Breitkopf & Härtel agree to publish his recent oratorio *Das Paradies und die Peri*, Op. 50. Härtel did not honor Schumann's request.

In December of 1844, hoping that new surroundings might improve Robert's declining condition, the Schumanns moved to Dresden. The spring brought about a gradual convalescence and in June, Schumann took up work on a "rondo in A major." Drafted in just three days, its completion was noted "with joy … beautiful day" on June 16.[55] On July 1 "began orchestration of the rondo," a process which took him considerably longer, not being finished until July 12.[56] That the rondo was conceived to complement the fantasy was confirmed by Clara in her diary on June 27: "Robert has composed a beautiful last movement to his fantasy for piano and orchestra, so that it has now become a concerto, which I will play next winter. I look greatly forward to it, as I have always desired a large-scale bravura piece from him."[57] Though the concerto might appear predestined for Clara, it was more likely Schumann's inability to find the fantasy a publisher that lay behind his decision to return to the earlier work and position it within a larger framework.

Completion of a second movement for the concerto on July 16 found Schumann "very happy."[58] And in the 13 days from July 17–29, during which time he was beset by illness, Schumann recast the fantasy as the concerto's first movement. The household book reports a "bad condition of nerves" on July 24,[59] followed by "ill" on both July 28 and 29 (the date entered in the manuscript [page 79, revised pagination] for completion of the first movement). On July 30 he household book reads "very ill."[60]

From the evidence provided by the autograph, it appears Schumann was especially concerned with orchestral clarity, paring what can be gleaned of the distinctly thicker orchestration of the original fantasy in preference of an almost chamberlike sonority (e.g., in the *Andante espressivo*). He also carried out several structural alterations that, as Stephen Roe has pointed out, suggest a concern with bringing the fantasy's freer structure more in line with that of a conventional concerto first movement.[61] The most noticeable revision involved replacing an eight-measure transition that preceded the *Andante espressivo* with a full orchestral tutti (measures 133–155). This caused Schumann to cross out the original page 23 and necessitated inserting another bifolium (two manuscript leaves), thereby disrupting the movement's original pagination. The Greek insertion sign ♪ (Di Gamma) was entered to connect the new musical text. Schumann also revised the solo part in the development section (measures 205–259) working the melody already assigned to the wind instruments into the piano's arpeggiated figures. In so doing, he rendered the passage considerably more difficult. Preferring not to copy this version into the manuscript, he simply placed the shorthand instruction "see piano part" in measure 205 (a reference to the separate solo performance score). A final alteration involved crossing out measures 439–444 in the copyist's hand, and replacing them with 12 new measures that now end the cadenza.

Clara was delighted. "Robert has completed his concerto and given it over to the copyist. "I am overjoyed at the prospect of playing it with orchestra,"[62] reads her diary entry for July 31. On the same day, the Schumanns set out for Bonn, planning to participate in a Beethoven celebration on August 10–12. Without reaching their intended destination, they turned back owing to Robert's deteriorating health. In their travel notes they placed the concerto among the list of works to be addressed upon their return to Dresden.[63]

Ferdinand Hiller, a close friend of the Schumanns, was the Concerto's dedicatee as well as the conductor at its premiere performance.

A premiere performance was arranged under the auspices of composer and conductor Ferdinand Hiller. Hiller had befriended the Schumanns in Dresden and drawn them into his circle of acquaintances. He also welcomed their participation in a series of subscription concerts he had organized. It was on the second program of the 1845–46 season that the concerto would be given its first hearing. Clara began study of the solo part on September 3,[64] playing it through several times at her father's house, recorded by Robert in the household book on September 9 ("evening rehearsal at the old man's … my concerto") and again on September 13, Clara's 26th birthday.[65] "Concert errands"[66] noted on November 28 likely included Schumann's correspondence with Hiller confirming that the "premiere will take place on the fourth, and the first orchestra rehearsal next Wednesday."[67] Schumann also discussed the other works that Clara would play on the program and her fee. "Concert worries"[68] reported in the household book on November 30 preceded the two morning rehearsals of December 3 and 4.

Robert-Schumann-Haus Zwickau; Archiv-Nr.: 10463-A3; Programmsammlung Clara Schumanns, Nr. 231

The concerto's premiere at 7:00 PM in the hall of Dresden's Hôtel de Saxe (the "Orchestra of the Subscription Concerts" conducted by Hiller) was poorly attended. This according to the critic in Leipzig's *Allgemeine Musikalische Zeitung,* who nonetheless gave the work an enthusiastic reception, "We have every reason to praise this composition very highly and to rank it among the composer's best works … [it] avoids the monotony of the usual concerti with both parts displaying independence in a beautiful whole … we would be hard pressed to decide which movement gave us the most pleasure."[69] In a similar vein the *Dresden Abendzeitung* commented that "it has been a long time since we have heard such an interesting piano composition as this concerto."[70]

DONNERSTAG DEN 4. DECEMBER 1845.

Concert

VON

Clara Schumann,

Kammervirtuosin Sr. Maj. des Kaisers von Oesterreich,

im Saale des Hôtel de Saxe in Dresden.

Erster Theil.

1) Lustspiel-Ouverture für Orchester v. F. Hiller (Manuscr.)
2) Concert für das Pianoforte mit Begleitung des Orchesters von R. Schumann, vorgetragen von **Clara Schumann.**
   Allegro affettuoso.
   Andantino und Rondo.
3) Arie, vorgetragen von Fräul. **Louise Franchetti.**
4) Ballade (as-dur) von F. Chopin, vorgetragen von **Clara Schumann.**

Zweiter Theil.

5) Ouverture, Scherzo und Finale für Orchester, von R. Schumann.
6) Duo zu vier Händen für das Pianoforte (Manuscript) von F. Mendelssohn-Bartholdy, vorgetragen von Herrn Musik-Director **F. Hiller** und **Clara Schumann.**
7) a) Die Lotosblume, von Heine,   } Lieder von R.
   b) Der Nussbaum, von J. Mosen, } Schumann,
   vorgetragen von Fräul. **Louise Franchetti.**
8) a) Fuge von S. Bach,
   b) Wiegenlied von A. Henselt,
   c) Lied ohne Worte (aus dem 6. Hefte) von F. Mendelssohn,
   vorgetragen von **Clara Schumann.**

Billets zu Sperrsitzen à 1 Thaler, sowie zu unnummerirten Sitzen à 20 Neugroschen sind in der Hof-Musikalienhandlung des Herrn Meser, Schlossgasse Nr. 9 zu haben. An der Kasse kostet das Billet zu einem Sperrsitze 1 Thlr. 10 Ngr. und zu einem unnummerirten Sitze 1 Thlr.

Anfang 7 Uhr.   Ende 9 Uhr.

Program from the premiere performance of the Concerto in Dresden on December 4, 1845. As was Schumann's desire, the Concerto is listed as having only two movements.

Again, balance was at issue, with the reviewer finding the work to be more an "instrumental fantasy with piano" than a true concerto. The *Neue Zeitschrift* was somewhat more critical. While pronouncing the last two movements most successful the critic found the first, owing to its frequent alternation between solo and tutti, rather difficult to comprehend.[71] The same journal proffered a more favorable view of the concerto when Alfred Dörfell reviewed the published score in 1847, declaring it "one of the greatest works of the past year."

*The depth and truth of feeling expressed makes our hearts beat faster, awaking
all blessed emotions one is capable of feeling, yearning for ideal inner peace,
conveying this peace, and letting us feel this peace ourselves. In the aura that
comes over us, we experience a joyful glow of the soul for everything that takes
us beyond the boundaries of this world and reveals a closeness to eternity.*[72]

Not long after the Dresden premiere Schumann wrote to Mendelssohn with the hope of
securing a more important performance in the musical center of Leipzig: "I would like to
tell you a few things about my concerto; but above all, I want you to hear it. Might that
still be possible at a subscription concert?"[73] Mendelssohn agreed and placed the concerto
on the eleventh program of the Gewandhaus season, New Year's Day, 1846. Schumann
expressed his gratitude to Mendelssohn in a letter of December 18,[74] to whom Clara also
wrote on December 27: "Is the rehearsal for the concert on Wednesday? If you should
hold it on Tuesday, however, I would like very much to rehearse the concerto then because
there is never enough time in the dress rehearsal for a single piece. The concerto is rather
difficult, so that we easily need over an hour for it. Please have the kindness to consider
this in arranging the rehearsal!"[75] According to an observer at one of the rehearsals
(composer Johann [Joseph Hermann] Verhulst, 1816–1891), things went poorly at first
and even fell apart in the last movement (beginning at measure 189).[76] Eventually all
was brought in order and the Leipzig performance was evidently successful enough to
convince a publisher (Härtel) to issue the work. Schumann informed Ferdinand Hiller
by letter the following day[77] and also dedicated the score to him.

Entry in the household book on January 16 of a word coined by Schumann *Concertveränd-
erungsqual* (concerto-alterations-ordeal) reveals that the score was subjected to a final
process of revision.[78] Forwarded to Härtel on January 21, receipt of the publication fee
(138 Thalers) was registered in the household book on January 24.[79] The first edition
appeared in July 1846 and was advertised for sale the following month in *Hofmeisters
Monatsbericht* (vol. 18).

As was his habit, Schumann catalogued the places and dates of numerous performances
on the fly leaf of his personal library copy. These included the Dresden (1845) and
Leipzig (1846) premieres, and subsequent performances in Vienna and Prague (the latter
two conducted by Schumann himself), Zwickau (July 10, 1847), Leipzig (April 6, 1848),
Cologne (1850), Hamburg (1850), Leipzig (1850), Frankfurt (n.d.), Rotterdam
(February 1853), Paris (April 3, 1853), and Stuttgart (1853). The last entered took place
on December 1, 1853 in Rotterdam where Clara performed the solo part: "I was greatly
moved by the whole affair," she recalled in her diary.[80] Undoubtedly, the Piano
Concerto in A Minor held a special place for Robert as well, as he wrote to Clara from
his terminal incarceration at the asylum in Endenich in the autumn of 1854:

*Now I should like to remind you of some things, of blessed times that have
passed, of our journeys to Switzerland, Heidelberg, Lausanne, Vevey,
Chamonix; our further travels to the Haag, where your accomplishments were
remarkable; and on to Antwerp and Brussels, and then the music festival in
Düsseldorf, where my Fourth Symphony [Op. 120] was heard for the first
time, and on the second day, the A Minor Concerto was presented, so gloriously
played by you, the applause resounding.*[81]

Analysis and Interpretation

When Schumann returned to the prior composed fantasy intent on placing it within a larger structure he posed himself a considerable architectural challenge. As the influential Viennese critic Eduard Hanslick (1825–1904) pointed out in his 1858 appraisal of the work, the concerto's first movement, with its succession of contrasting tempi, established of itself a "miniature representation of a concerto."[82] Such a state of affairs would make it necessary for Schumann to find the means not only of integrating the fantasy within a larger context but of countering its weight in the concerto's complementary movements.

Schumann's apt solution was to effect a seamless transition between the second and third movements, in effect creating a two-part structure of appropriate length and emphasis to balance the tripartite impression given by the first movement. For Schumann, the finished concerto had two movements, and he was clearly concerned that it be perceived as such when he wrote to Mendelssohn (shortly before the Leipzig premiere) that "my concerto is divided into *Allegro affettuoso*, *Andantino* and *Rondo*—the last two are elided—perhaps you could note that on the program."[83] The evidence provided by the autograph manuscript makes clear that the connection between the *Andantino* and *Rondo* was a trying exercise for the composer.[84]

Schumann's original conception, still visible in the autograph, involved a single E (measure 102) sustained in the first violins, followed by a general pause and a double bar. Although a somewhat curious ending for a movement in F major, it did serve to establish a tonal relationship to the A major Finale, to which the inscription *Attaca Rondo* (later crossed out) directed a close link. Apparently not satisfied (the date of "July 16, 1845" given for completion of the movement can also be seen struck out beneath the horn part), Schumann then conceived a new six measure transition (measures 103–108). A bold "**X**" scrawled in crayon over the new material served temporarily to restore the original conception. Some time later, attempted erasure of the crayon marking and placement of the word "Gilt" (stet), underlined twice, indicated a further change of heart.

This remarkable page from the autograph manuscript speaks to the difficulty Schumann experienced in creating the magical transition from the Intermezzo to the Finale. The large cross (drawn in red/brown crayon, which Schumann later tried unsuccessfully to erase) is still visible and reveals one of several changes of mind.

Courtesy of the Heinrich-Heine-Institut, Düsseldorf

With the transition now restored Schumann found it necessary to alter the opening passage of the *Allegro vivace*. Bringing forward the ascending octave scales heard in the transition (string parts, measures 107–108) he composed the eight measures that open the Finale and provide a brief anticipation of the theme proper. With the addition of this material, on a single sheet of paper affixed in the manuscript and explained with "Vi/de"[85] marks, the transition reached the final form in which it comes down to us.

Schumann also sought out the broader means by which to establish unity throughout the concerto. In his earlier symphonic works he had already explored the possibilities of subtle thematic connections and inter-quotation between movements (particularly in the D minor symphony of 1841, later revised and published as his Fourth Symphony, Op. 120). In the concerto, this concentration on limited means is at once apparent in the relationship between the principal theme of the opening *Allegro affettuoso* movement, and that of the *Allegro vivace*. Both share a similar range and contour (falling at the interval of a third, then rising a fifth).

Schumann: Op. 54, Allegro affettuoso *(measures 4–7)*

Schumann: Op. 54, Allegro vivace *(measures 117–120)*

And the principal thematic ideas of the concerto's three movements all share a rhythmic gesture, a further example of preoccupation with organic integrity.

Schumann: Op. 54, Allegro affettuoso *(measures 5–6)*

Schumann: Op. 54, Intermezzo *(pickup and measure 1)*

Schumann: Op. 54, Allegro vivace *(measures 110–111)*

Any discussion of the concerto's content must necessarily give consideration to the designation Schumann had attached to the earlier realization of its first movement: fantasy. Although in widespread use in the early part of the 19th century, the designation was rather uncommon for a concertante work. Fortunately, Schumann explained his concept of the term. A fantasy, he contended, should enjoy a basic freedom of form, while possessing an "inner thread, which should also shine through the fantastic disorder."[86] For Schumann, the free associations brought by the term should be contained through some underlying means of formal organization. In the fantasy of 1841, this was brought about through concentration on a limited fund of thematic ideas. By way of example, Schumann's secondary theme (measures 59 ff.) is little more than a transposition (into C major) of the first.

For Schumann, the term fantasy may have also welcomed a programmatic association. His best-known use of the designation—the remarkable solo piano Fantasie, Op. 17 of 1838—is explicitly programmatic. Schumann not only prefaced that score with an enigmatic quotation of Friedrich von Schlegel (1772–1829), but placed thinly veiled references to the sixth and final song of Beethoven's song cycle *An die ferne Geliebte*, Op. 98, in the score. Although there is nothing in Schumann's own literature to suggest it, some commentators have singled out other elements in the concerto which might well point to a program. Arnfried Edler has noted the close kinship between the principal theme of the concerto's first movement (as it appears in the *Andante espressivo*) and the opening of Florestan's aria "In des Lebens Frühlingstagen" (In the Springtime of My Life), which begins the second act of Beethoven's opera *Fidelio*.[87]

Beethoven: Fidelio, *Act 2, No. 11*

Schumann: Op. 54, Andante espressivo *(measures 156–158)*

At this moment Florestan, languishing in a Seville prison, has a near delirious vision of an angel, which he likens to his wife, Leonore. As was so often the case with Schumann's earlier works, Clara would appear to supply the inspiration here. Schumann was acquainted with *Fidelio*, having attended performances of it in 1838, and more immediate to the fantasy's conception, with Clara on April 5, 1840.

Egon Voss, in his commentary on the concerto, also found Clara to be a likely source of inspiration. He proposed that the first four notes of the principal theme might represent a sort of *soggetto cavato*,[88] with their German spelling C-H-A-A (C-B-A-A being the English equivalent) outlining "Chiara," Schumann's affectionate name for Clara in his mythical society of *Davidsbund*.[89] Gerd Nauhaus has also brought to light a similarity between a figure in the first movement of Clara's Sonata in G Minor (given to Robert as a Christmas present in 1841) and one found in the concerto's Intermezzo.

Clara Schumann: Piano Sonata in G Minor, first movement (measure 67)

Schumann: Op. 54, Intermezzo (measure 11)

A further possible alliance with Clara's work is also forged in the Intermezzo. The prominence given the cello recalls the slow movement of Clara's youthful concerto of 1833–34.

The concerto's first movement commences with a four-measure fanfare-like introduction, which is followed by statements of the lyrical principal theme, first by orchestra (measures 4–11), then soloist (measures 12–19). A transition (pickup to measure 20–58) brings us to the secondary thematic group (measures 59–134), with the exposition then brought to a close by an orchestral tutti (pickup to 133–155). Schumann begins the development section with a change of tempo and meter (*Andante espressivo*, measure 156 ff.), presenting yet another variant of the principal theme. A return to the prior *Allegro* tempo (measure 185) involves manipulation of the opening fanfare, and leads to an extended passage (marked *Passionato*, measure 205 ff.) that relies heavily on the sort of sequential episodes that Schumann so favored in his development sections.

The recapitulation (a slightly truncated account of the exposition) begins at measure 259, closing with an orchestral tutti (this time with piano obligato, pickup to measure 385–398) that leads directly into the cadenza. No longer customary since the time of Beethoven, Schumann's incorporation of a cadenza at the traditionally prescribed moment represents a revival of sorts. In his article "The Piano Concerto," Schumann had considered "the old cadenza in which virtuosi of times past incorporated every possible bravura effect,"[90] opting for one, completely written out, that affords little opportunity for technical display. The coda, based on a rhythmic variant of the principal theme, proceeds in a tempo (*Allegro molto*, measure 458) considerably faster than the movement's overall pace. A number of accelerando effects, which were later crossed out by the composer, are still visible in the autograph manuscript—*sempre stringendo* (at measures 470 and 490) and *Più presto* (measure 516).

The Intermezzo is cast in ternary (**A B A**) form and is almost Mozartean in its simplicity and grace. In the first part (measures 1–28), a motive in the piano solo (beginning on beat 2 of measure 6), bears a subtle relation to the cantabile cello line that opens the **B** part (beginning with the pickup to measure 29–68.

Schumann: Op. 54, Intermezzo (piano solo, measures 6–7)

Schumann: Op. 54, Intermezzo (cello, measures 28–31)

A modified return to the first part (pickup to measures 69–102) is followed by the transitional passage (measures 103–108), which connects directly to the closing *Allegro vivace*. Although *attaca* movements had become quite commonplace in concerti, what distinguishes Schumann's transition is the remarkable way in which he harks back to the principal theme of the concerto's opening movement (with the descending chords in the piano vaguely reminiscent of the concerto's opening fanfare) while anticipating that of the Finale. In this regard, the closest relative appears to be Beethoven's Fifth Piano Concerto, Op. 73, a work that Clara had added to her repertoire in 1844 and was undoubtedly fresh in his mind.[91]

The final movement (*Allegro vivace*) was originally referred to by Schumann as a rondo, though he later crossed out the designation at all points in the manuscript except on the fly leaf and (perhaps inadvertently) over the horn part (measure 105). Nonetheless, he occasionally preserved the designation—in the project book[92] and on the first program—and the movement's larger sonata form does embrace many elements common to the rondo.

Courtesy of the Heinrich-Heine-Institut, Düsseldorf

This autograph manuscript page from the Finale juxtaposes Clara Schumann's handwriting in the solo part with that of Robert in the orchestral parts. While Clara's clefs and rests are somewhat dissimilar, the most marked difference is in the placement of downward stems—Clara's are invariably on the right of the note head (see the left-hand octaves in the solo part), whereas Robert's are on the left. Robert placed the orientation numbers above the solo part to indicate a literal recapitulation of earlier material (here transposed up a fourth). These 210 measures copied out by Clara constitute her largest contribution to the manuscript.

An eight-measure introduction (pickup to measures 109–116) precedes the full statement of the jubilant principal theme/rondo refrain (pickup to measures 116–148). Transitional material (pickup to measures 149–189) leads to the secondary thematic group (measures 189–327) with its challenging hemiola effect. The development section, beginning at measure 359, includes a brief fugato (measures 367 ff.), which quite possibly reflects the renewed interest in counterpoint Schumann had shown in the spring of 1845 (and which also yielded such contrapuntal exercises as the *Studies*, Op. 56, *Sketches*, Op. 58, and the organ fugue on *B-A-C-H*, Op. 60, No. 1). The main body of the development introduces a new theme (beginning with the pickup to measure 392), which is followed in characteristic fashion by a host of sequential passages (pickup to measures 414–484). A transition (measures 485–496) leads to the recapitulation, which takes place in the unexpected subdominant key of D major (at measure 497). A final statement of the principal theme, once again back in A major (measures 739–770), is followed by a coda (measures 771–979). Here Schumann draws freely on the transitional material of the exposition, fragments of the main theme, the fugato, and the new theme introduced in the development.

In a sense, Schumann's Piano Concerto in A Minor defies any sort of traditional analysis. It relies no more on the Classical distribution of tutti and solo sections than it looks to its contemporaries for models. By the summer of 1845 Schumann was an accomplished, if largely self-taught, composer who had overcome his early lack of formal, systematic training. The Piano Concerto in A Minor, with its remarkable organic unity forged from a fund of limited melodic means, exudes Schumann's inimitable blend of youthful vigor and innate lyricism. No wonder Hanslick remarked that "one does not have to conclude from the opus number [54] that this was created in the master's most productive and favorable period."[93]

About This Edition

The text of the present edition is based on the autograph manuscript (which, until 1989, had rested for 144 years in private possession) and the composer's own copy of the first printed edition. The task of discovering Schumann's final intentions with regard to the score is challenging on several accounts. As detailed below, the autograph manuscript for the concerto is not a *Stichvorlage* (the kind of meticulously prepared fair copies that Schumann typically prepared for use by an engraver) but rather reflects a composition still in the working stages. Nor does the first printed edition present the concerto in highly polished form either. Governed by economic constraints (a desire to impress as much music as possible on each plate), many of the tempo, dynamic, expressive and pedal markings were moved, appear misaligned, or in some instances, were likely left out altogether when space did not permit. For these reasons, a great many inconsistencies, errors and oversights arise both within and amongst these primary sources. Few involve errors of pitch—a notable exception is found at the opening of the Intermezzo, where the manuscript and first edition are clearly at odds (see the discussion in the Critical Commentary concerning measure 1 of the Intermezzo).

The greatest challenge was in reconciling the numerous discrepancies that arise with regard to articulation and expressive markings between analogous passages—as much a reflection of the more casual editing standards of the 19th century as that of Schumann's own apparent comfort with subtle incongruities in the score. Those issues, which have been brought into general agreement, are noted in the Critical Commentary. The score was also further clarified through comparison with the two editions prepared under the editorial guidance of Schumann's wife Clara. In certain instances, archaic notation has been adjusted to conform with modern practice. Any purely editorial additions to the score that might prove useful to the performer have been placed in parentheses.

FINGERING. No fingering was placed in the autograph manuscript and a scant four numbers (in the final movement, measures 320 and 322) represent the only fingering published in the first printed edition. As these numbers correspond to those found in Clara Schumann's *Instruktive Ausgabe* (Instructive Edition) they were presumably drawn from the original performance part. With this single exception, all fingering supplied here is by the editor.

A number of passages in the concerto are unwieldy for pianists with smaller reaches. In some instances Schumann may have intended that larger chords be rolled. At one such point in the first movement (measure 118) the autograph manuscript has an arpeggio mark prefacing the left-hand chord. This is not reproduced in the first edition, or at any subsequent passage in the autograph. Pianists with smaller hands may find it necessary to roll or break this, and similar such chords. To assist the pianist, fingering has also been added to the orchestral reduction. Where alternate fingerings are offered, they appear together, separated by a horizontal line.

PEDALING. Schumann's directions for the pedal are at times general (e.g., the indication *sempre con pedale* found in the concerto's first movement at measure 156), other times specific (carefully placed signs that call for more precise effects). Schumann deemed the latter to be necessary only in certain passages, expounding his approach in a footnote supplied to the first edition of his Piano Sonata No. 1 in F-sharp Minor, Op. 11: "The authors [meaning Florestan and Eusebius] use the pedal in almost every measure, according to circumstances required by the harmonies. Those exceptions, where they wish the pedal not to be used, are marked with ⊕ ; then, when the indication *Pedale* reappears, the continual use of the pedal resumes."[94] A contemporaneous account of Schumann's playing also confirms that he relied heavily on use of the damper pedal: "It sounded as if the sustaining pedal was always halfway down, so that the sonorities flowed into one another."[95] Although Schumann placed a rather large number of specific pedal instructions in the concerto, it can be safely assumed that he anticipated liberal use of the damper pedal even when any such signs are absent. With the exception of a few instances where use of the pedal seems warranted by comparison with analogous passages, only Schumann's original pedal markings are reproduced here. In the concerto's second movement, the indication *mit Verschiebung*, found in measure 106, refers to an "off-setting" of the mechanism by the far left pedal (found on the newer Hammerklaviers of Schumann's time[96]) and is equivalent to the soft pedal on modern instruments.

ORNAMENTATION. The single grace note is by far the most common ornament found in Schumann's piano writing. Oftentimes its function is purely ornamental, adding a trace of color to passage work (e.g., in the Finale at measures 256, 260, 270, 274, etc.). Other times, it is incorporated as an indispensable part of the musical idea (e.g., the numerous occurrences in the Intermezzo, where it forms part of the melodic ideas). Another favored device is to use it to place emphasis or draw attention to a moment of special importance, whether forceful (as in the opening of the Second Piano Sonata, Op. 22) or more subtle (prefacing statements in the solo part of the concerto's primary and secondary themes, measure 12 and measures 58–59). In all cases, grace notes should precede the beat and their speed be determined by the context of the passage.

In a like manner, Schumann used short trills (⤳) in the concerto as decoration (e.g., in the coda of the Finale at measures 778, 786, ff.) or to impart emphasis (as in the first movement at measures 40 and 46). The long trill was not an effect especially favored by Schumann. In very few instances did he rely on the device to serve in an important structural capacity (e.g., in the Fantasie, Op. 17, first movement, measures 24–27, where it fulfills a harmonic function and contributes to the urgency of the material). In the concerto, trills appear in the traditional manner of pure embellishment (e.g., in the cadenza at measures 434–438 and elsewhere), often appearing at the penultimate moment of an extended passage (in the Finale at measures 347–358 and measures 727–738). Some editors have added terminations to the trills in the Finale, but there is no reason to suggest their inclusion is either necessary or warranted by tradition. Trills should begin on the principal note.

On occasion, Schumann places his melodic material in smaller notes where he calls for a freedom of execution contrary to strict rhythmic notation (e.g., in the first movement at measures 65 and 115). Such passages should be performed in a rhythmically free manner.

Robert-Schumann-Haus Zwickau; o. Archiv-Nr.   Photo: Ferdinand Franz, Zwickau

Photo of the Memorial Room in the Robert-Schumann-Haus in Zwickau. This room was provided with historical furniture formerly owned by the Schumann family and thus obtains the character of a special memorial room.

METRONOME MARKINGS. Considerable controversy surrounds the metronome markings that Schumann placed in his scores, much of it inadvertently occasioned by Clara Schumann herself, who saw fit to alter a number of them for her editions. This has lent some credence to the notion that his metronome was itself at fault, even though the composer had carefully tested its accuracy and declared in a letter to composer Ferdinand Böhme (1815–1883) that "mine is correct."[97] Moreover, while Clara did make noticeable changes to some of Robert's markings, she retained the vast majority of them. And among those works that she did alter, there can be seen no consistent pattern of deviation in the direction of either faster or slower tempi, something one might reasonably presume in the case of a defective metronome.[98]

Although Clara did not effect any changes in her editions to Schumann's original markings for the concerto, they still bear scrutiny. The designation of ♩ = 84 for the opening *Allegro affettuoso* is considerably faster than the performance tradition. So is the marking of ♩. = 72 for the ensuing *Andante espressivo* (measure 156). Even more striking is his provision of that identical marking (♩. = 72) for the concerto's final *Allegro vivace* (measure 109). It may have been Schumann's intention, in assigning so rapid a pace for the *Andante espressivo*, to somewhat obscure the disparate sections of the original fantasy. On a broader scale, it is not unreasonable to suppose that Schumann's decision to assign the same metronome marking to both the *Andante espressivo* and *Allegro vivace* is symbolic of a further effort to find unity in the concerto through means of tempo. Nonetheless, as is always the case, metronome markings should be only considered for the general guidance that they provide, and no doubt in Schumann's case, the performer can comfortably exercise considerable latitude in establishing a tempo.

Robert-Schumann-Haus Zwickau; Archiv-Nr.: 4302–B2

Clara and Robert Schumann (1859); steel engraving based on daguerreotype from 1850.

Sources Used in Preparation of This Edition

Primary Sources

AUTOGRAPH MANUSCRIPT

The only early source that appears to have survived for the work, the autograph of the Piano Concerto in A Minor is a working manuscript. As such, it has as much to reveal about Schumann's creative process as it does about the complex origins of the concerto itself. The manuscript's 192 pages, in oblong format (the solo part always found at the top of the score), display Schumann's characteristic use of various writing implements: ink (umber), pencil and crayon (red/brown). It is heavily revised by the composer, with a large number of alterations, erasures and corrections entered in the score. Bound in green marbled board, with a fly leaf placed at the front and back, each movement is individually paginated, befitting a work whose constituent parts were composed out of sequence. Gold-embossed lettering on the spine reads: "Concert für Pianoforte."

From a technical standpoint, the manuscript is not entirely autograph, as the presence of two other hands is visible in the score. Schumann employed a copyist (as was his habit since the mid-1830s) in the preparation of the manuscript, in this case the Dresden musician Karl Mehner (d. 1878 or later) who had also served on occasion as a copyist for Richard Wagner (1813–1883). Working from the since-lost manuscript (or solo performance parts) of the prior-composed fantasy, Mehner laid out the pages and wrote in the solo part for most of the concerto's first movement.[99] Schumann then filled in the orchestration and added cue notes to the soloist's system, anticipating its use as both a study score for the pianist, and lead score for the conductor.

Clara Schumann's distinctive handwriting is also visible in all three movements of the concerto (in the solo and orchestral parts). Clara was charged primarily with copying out recapitulatory passages, most extensively in the final movement (measures 529–739), which involved transposition a fourth higher from the corresponding text (measures 149–359). There is nothing unusual in Clara Schumann's involvement with the manuscript as she frequently assisted with copying and arranging her husband's work.

FIRST PRINTED EDITION (COMPOSER'S PERSONAL COPY)

The first printed edition, issued by Breitkopf & Härtel in July 1846 (plate nos. 7413 [solo part] and 7415 [orchestral parts]) was prepared not from the autograph manuscript, but from the original performance parts (since lost or otherwise unaccounted for). This according to Schumann's correspondence of January 21, 1846 to Hermann Härtel: "With many thanks for your friendly cooperation I shall send you today my piano concerto. Hopefully it will reward you for all the interest in my efforts that you have shown. The orchestral parts will follow in a few days."[100] The composer's copy,[101] bound for his personal library, lacks both price and plate number on the title page, and is therefore presumably a pre-publication print. A small number of corrections entered in pencil confirm that Schumann reviewed the score, and serve to establish its primacy as a source for the concerto. Nonetheless, he overlooked a number of errors and inconsistencies, perpetuated not only in the edition for two pianos brought out by the same publisher in 1861 (which employed the same engraving of the solo part as the first edition[102]), but in many other subsequent editions as well. A full score did not appear in print until six years after the composer's death, when justified by sufficient sales (Leipzig: Breitkopf & Härtel, 1862, plate no. 10317).

The title page (above) from Schumann's personal copy of the first printed edition of the Concerto (Leipzig: Breitkopf & Härtel, 1846). On the fly leaf (right) a number of performances attended by Schumann are entered in his own hand.

Secondary Sources

Also consulted for comparison purposes were the two editions published under the editorship of Clara Schumann. The Collected Works (Leipzig: Breitkopf & Härtel, 1881–93), series III, *Concerte und Concertstücke für Orchester*, contains the concerto in full score. Although Clara relied on the assistance of a rather large number of individuals in the preparation of this edition (most notably Johannes Brahms) she is listed solely as editor.

The Instructive Edition (Leipzig: Breitkopf & Härtel, 1887) contains only the works for piano. It was revised after Clara's death by Carl Reinecke (1824–1910) and a number of reprints and revisions have appeared in other languages as well. It is commonly known in English as *The Complete Works for Piano Solo, Edited According to Manuscripts and from her Personal Recollections by Clara Schumann.*[103] In keeping with the nature of so-called instructive editions, which were drawn up to illustrate a particular performer's interpretive ideas, there is a fair amount of editorial intrusion. Clara added numerous tempo, dynamic, expressive and pedal indications to the score.

Although the editions of Clara Schumann have been criticized for their lack of scholarly apparatus, their importance should not be discounted. She was the concerto's first interpreter, and her performances were heralded by Schumann and others. As the noted pianist and conductor Hans von Bülow (1830–1894) observed in the *Berliner Feuerspritze*, "when the compositions of the greatest modern orchestral composers are interpreted with such wonderful perfection, with such soaring conception of the whole, and such elaborate shading of detail, they make way to reach even the most reluctant and skeptical audience. Schumann's Piano Concerto in A Minor was heard to best advantage through the performance of this great master [Clara]."[104]

Dedicated in Friendship to Ferdinand Hiller

PIANO CONCERTO IN A MINOR

for Piano Solo and Orchestra (Arranged for Second Piano)

Robert Schumann (1810–1856)
Op. 54

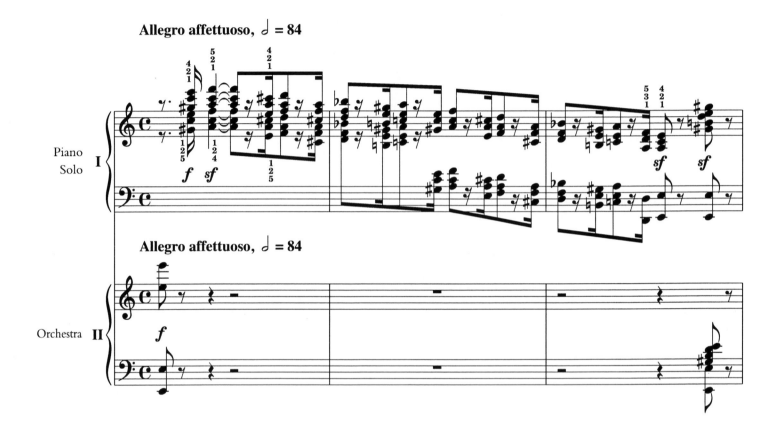

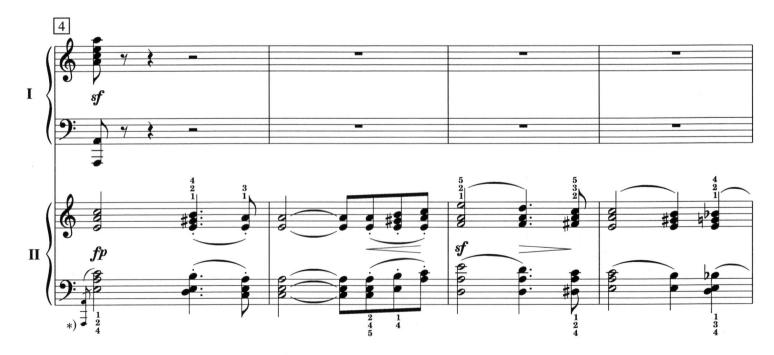

*) All grace notes are played before the beat unless otherwise indicated.

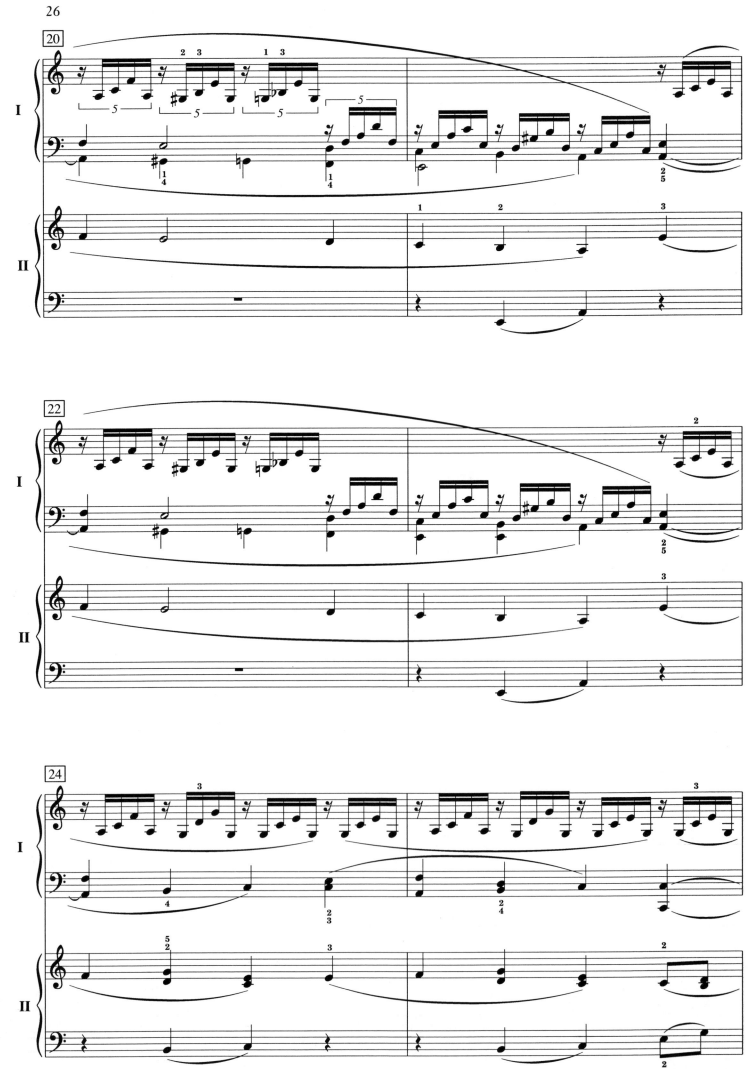

*) The trill may be played either before the beat or on the beat at the performer's discretion.

*) The accents on the last note of certain triplet groups, which appear with some consistency in the autograph, may not have actually been intended as accents. Rather, it was likely that Schumann simply meant to ensure that this weakest note of the triplet would be played with the same tone as the others, owing to the exchange of hands.

*) The autograph manuscript has an arpeggio mark prefacing the left-hand chord. It is not reproduced in the first edition or at any subsequent passage in the manuscript. Pianists with smaller reaches may find it necessary to break this and similar large chords.

*) Pianists with smaller reaches may find it expedient to rearrange this
passage, taking the upper left-hand notes with the right hand as follows:

etc.

II (Orchestra)

I (Piano Solo)

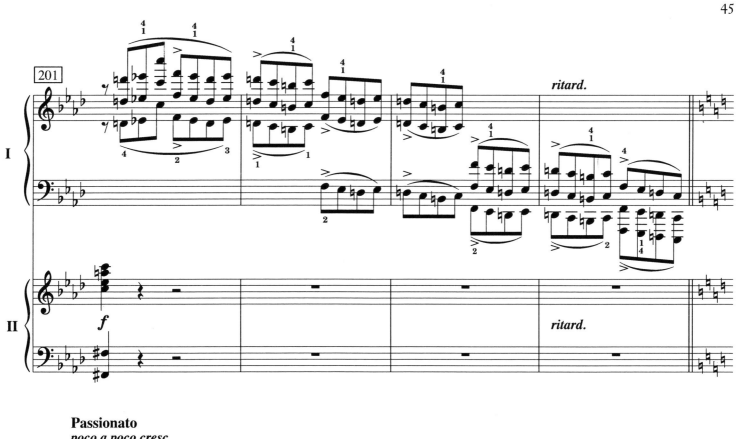

*) In a relatively late change to the score, Schumann decided to incorporate the melody into what had previously been a mere accompaniment figure in the solo part.

Measures 205–208 as found in the autograph manuscript:

In measure 205 he simply wrote *"s. Clavierstim[m]e"* ("see piano part"), referring to the solo performance part (since lost or otherwise unaccounted for). The new version not only rendered the passage considerably more difficult, but owing to the rhythmic complexities, at times the melody is staggered against its counterpart in the orchestral part.

*) See footnote to measure 128.

Cadenza

*) This trill may begin on the upper note to match the beginning of the RH trill.

*) There is no pedal release in any of the primary sources.

INTERMEZZO
Andantino grazioso, ♪ = 120

*) The cascading passage through measure 189 can be played either entirely by the RH, or measure 188 can be divided between the hands, as shown in the score. (This also applies to the passage at measures 566–569.)

*) Begin the trill on the principal note. A temination is neither necessary nor warranted by tradition; however, an optional termination may help facilitate the transition from the trill in measure 358 to a firm downbeat in measure 359. This also applies to the analogous passage in measures 727–739.

I (Piano Solo)

I (Piano Solo)

II (Orchestra)

I (Piano Solo)

Critical Commentary

Table of Abbreviations:

AM   Autograph Manuscript

FE   First Printed Edition, Lead Score (Composer's Personal Copy)

CW   Collected Works Edition (Edited by Clara Schumann)

IE   Instructive Edition (Edited by Clara Schumann)

Measure   Comment

I. *Allegro affettuoso*

3–4   According to AM the RH solo part is as follows:

Schumann: Op. 54, measure 4 as found in FE.

It is entirely possible that this logical completion of the soloist's entrance represents the passage as it appeared in the Fantasy of 1841. At other points in the AM, where confusion might arise, Schumann took the trouble to write *große Noten* (large notes) or *mit kleineren Noten* (with small notes) to distinguish the solo part from the orchestral cue notes. Nevertheless, on the basis of FE, CW and IE, the solo part and orchestral cue notes seem reversed here in AM.

39   AM has *ff*; *f* according to FE, corresponding to that in orchestral parts at m. 41. Likewise, *ff* in solo part at analogous m. 294 corresponds to that in orchestral parts at m. 296.

45–47   Staccato marks absent in AM and FE; however, they are present in AM and FE at all analogous passages (mm. 39–41; 294–296; 300–302).

48   *espressivo* according to FE; absent in AM. Staccato marks for LH, beat 2 according to CW; absent in AM and FE here and at analogous m. 303.

56–57   CW and IE continue here the articulation voiced in mm. 48–56; these markings are absent from beat 4 onward here, and in the analogous passage (mm. 309–310) in both AM and FE.

58   FE has *p* here, added in pencil (not at analogous m. 311); absent in AM, CW and IE.

64   AM has *p*; absent in FE, CW and IE.

120   *sempre crescendo* according to FE; absent in AM.

156   *sempre con pedale* according to FE and CW; absent in AM and IE.

267   *p* according to AM; absent in FE, CW and IE. However, FE has *p* in the orchestral cue notes given at m. 259.

303   See note to m. 48.

309–310   See note to mm. 56–57.

349   Crescendo according to CW; absent in AM and FE (cf. analogous passage m. 96).

363–364 Grace note pickup to m. 364 absent in FE; this is clearly an oversight (cf. analogous passage mm. 110–111). The grace note is found in AM (though barely legible, especially as there is a page break between mm. 363 and 364 and it was Schumann's practice to place such grace notes in the *preceding* measure).

374 Diminuendo according to CW; absent in AM and FE (cf. analogous passage m. 121).

376 Diminuendo according to CW; absent in AM and FE (cf. analogous passage m. 123).

440 FE has ♯ before the trill sign (an obvious error); absent in AM.

483, 485, 487 *f* according to FE, CW and IE; absent in AM.

507 Pedal release added here; absent in AM and FE.

516 AM has **pp**, corresponding to that in orchestra; absent in FE, CW and IE.

II. Intermezzo. *Andantino grazioso*

1 AM clearly has F in place of E in the RH lower voice for the second 16th of beat 2; FE, CW and IE have E.

Schumann: Op. 54, Intermezzo, measure 1, RH as found in AM.

Unfortunately, the analogous passage in the reprise (m. 59 ff.) is not copied out in AM, though Schumann's placement of corresponding orientation numbers above the score indicates he intended a literal reprise. It is difficult to arrive at a definitive decision regarding Schumann's intentions here. The E could easily have been a mistake in the original performance part, perpetuated in FE and other subsequent editions (including those of Clara Schumann). It is especially perplexing when the orchestral interjections of the same musical gesture are taken into account: at mm. 17, 18 and 85, violin II has F. On the basis of FE, CW and IE, E is favored here and in the reprise; there can be no doubt that this was how Clara performed the passage.

13 Pedal release according to AM; absent in FE.

69 See note to Intermezzo m. 1.

106 Pedal release according to FE; absent in AM. Since there is no prior 🎵 indication to apply here, this possibly refers to release of the soft pedal in preparation for the *Allegro vivace*.

Allegro vivace

118 CW has staccato for the last three eighth notes; absent in AM and FE.

144 Accents according to AM; absent in FE. CW gives *sf*.

144 FE and CW have a quarter note in the alto voice on beat 1; it is changed to a dotted half note here according to analogous m. 128 and IE.

147–148 Accents according to AM.

184 Crescendo according to AM and FE; absent in CW.

215 *(simile)* added here to indicate continuation of RH articulation found in mm. 213–214.

256–258　The indication *sempre Pedale* in AM and FE. This indicates continuance of the pedaling noted in mm. 252–255.

359　FE has LH E octave in orchestral cue notes. However, this octave clearly belongs to the solo part, confirmed in CW and IE.

443–444　Pedal according to CW; absent in AM and FE (cf. mm. 439–440).

451–452　Pedal according to CW; absent in AM and FE.

453　AM has *sf* on beat 1; absent in FE.

455–456　Pedal according to CW; absent in AM and FE.

474, 478　℗ (which appears on beat 1 in AM and FE) is moved here to beat 2 of m. 475. This brings the indication in line with Schumann's previous pedal markings for all analogous passages (cf. mm. 414, 419 and 439).

523, 524　Staccato added by analogy with mm. 127–128.

595　*(simile)* added here to indicate continuation of the RH articulation found in mm. 593–594.

632　*p* according to AM; absent in FE.

710　*ff* according to AM and CW; FE has *f*.

711　*sf* according to FE; absent in AM.

737　Staccato on beat 3 absent in AM and FE; added by analogy with m. 735.

863　The sign ↝ according to AM, FE and IE; absent in CW.

863–864　Crescendo and diminuendo according to AM; absent in FE.

911　Accent according to CW; absent in AM and FE.

915–916　Accents according to AM; absent in FE.

923　Accent according to CW; absent in AM and FE.

Notes to the Text

[1]Sotheby's Auction Catalog "Cecilia" (Oxford: Nuffield Press, 1989), 139 (lot no. 207).

[2]Acquisition no. 89.5027 T.G. A facsimile of the autograph manuscript has been published in the series *Documenta Musicologica*: Zweite Reihe: Handschriften-Faksimiles 28 (Kassel: Bärenreiter, 1996).

[3]Robert Schumann, *Projektenbuch* ("Compositionsübersicht"), Archive of the Robert-Schumann-Haus (Zwickau), no. 4871/VII C,8–A3, 43.

[4]Robert Schumann, *Tagebücher*, vol. 1 (1827–38), ed. Georg Eisman (Leipzig: VEB Deutscher Verlag für Musik, 1971), 157 (December 16–17, 1828).

[5]See *Skizzenbuch III* (formerly Wiede 11/301c) now Bonn University Library, Mus. ms. autogr. R. Schumann *15*, 119; and *Skizzenbuch V* (formerly Wiede 11/301e) now Bonn University Library, Mus. ms. autogr. R. Schumann *17*, 13.

[6]Georg Eisman, *Robert Schumann: Ein Quellenwerk über sein Leben und Schaffen*, vol. 1 (Leipzig: Breitkopf & Härtel, 1956), 63.

[7]*Projektenbuch* ("Compositionsübersicht"), 44.

[8]*Tagebücher*, 1:360–62.

[9]See Claudia Macdonald, *Robert Schumann's F Major Concerto of 1831 as Reconstructed from his First Sketchbook: A History of its Composition and Study of its Musical Background* (Ph.D. diss., The University of Chicago, 1986), 9.

[10]*Tagebücher*, 1:315–16.

[11]Reinhard Kapp, *Studien zum Spätwerk Robert Schumanns* (Tutzing: Hans Schneider, 1984), 23–24.

[12]*Briefe: Neue Folge*, 32 (August 20, 1831).

[13]*Robert Schumann. Manuskripte. Briefe. Schumanniana*, Musikantiquariat Hans Schneider, catalog no. 188 (Tutzing: Hans Schneider, 1974), 79.

[14]Robert Schumann, *Jugendbriefe*, ed. Clara Schumann, 4th ed. (Leipzig: Breitkopf & Härtel, 1910), 194.

[15]Reproduced in Wolfgang Boetticher, *Robert Schumanns Klavierwerke: Neue biographische und textkritische Untersuchungen Teil I: Opus 1–6* (Wilhelmshaven: Heinrichshofen's Verlag, 1976), 37.

[16]Käthe Walch-Schumann, *Friedrich Wieck. Briefe aus den Jahren 1830–1838* (Cologne: Arno Volk-Verlag, 1968), 87.

[17]"Von K. [sic] Schumann. Ein Opus II," *Allgemeine Musikalische Zeitung* 33 (December 7, 1831), 807.

[18]"Pianoforte. Concerte," *Neue Zeitschrift für Musik* IV, no. 27 (April 1, 1836), 111.

[19]"Das Clavier-Concert," *Neue Zeitschrift für Musik* X, no. 2 (January 4, 1839), 5.

[20]Claudia Macdonald, "'Mit einer eignen außerordentlichen Composition:' The Genesis of Schumann's Phantasie in A Minor," *The Journal of Musicology* 12 (1995), 24 (note 17).

[21]"Schwärmbriefe An Chiara (No. 3)," *Neue Zeitschrift für Musik* III, no. 38 (November 10, 1835), 151.

[22]Ludwig Rellstab, *Gesammelte Schriften*, vol. 10 (Leipzig: F. A. Brockhaus, 1843), 213.

[23]"Das Clavier-Concert," *Neue Zeitschrift für Musik* X, no. 2 (January 4, 1839), 5.

[24]Clara and Robert Schumann, *Briefwechsel*, vol. 2, ed. Eva Weissweiler (Basel: Stroemfeld/Roter Stern, 1987), 358.

[25]Ibid., 2:361 (January 19, 1839).

[26]Ibid., 2:367.

[27]Robert Schumann, *Konzertsatz für Klavier und Orchester*, d-moll, reconstructed and completed by Jozef De Beenhouwer, ed. Joachim Draheim (Wiesbaden: Breitkopf & Härtel, [1988]), ix.

[28]*Briefwechsel*, 2:397.

[29]Robert Schumann, *Tagebücher*, vol. 2 (1836–54), ed. Gerd Nauhaus (Leipzig: VEB Deutscher Verlag für Musik, 1987), 122 (November 1840).

[30]*Projektenbuch*, 14.

[31]Alfred Dörfell, *Geschichte der Gewandhausconcerte zu Leipzig* (Leipzig: Breitkopf & Härtel, 1884; reprint, Leipzig: VEB Deutscher Verlag für Musik, 1980), 96.

[32]*Tagebücher*, 2:162 (May 2–9, 1841).

[33]Robert Schumann, *Tagebücher*, vol. 3 (*Haushaltbücher*), ed. Gerd Nauhaus (Leipzig: VEB Deutscher Verlag für Musik, 1982), 182.

[34]*Tagebücher*, 2:164 (May 10–22, 1841).

[35]"Pianoforte. Concerte," *Neue Zeitschrift für Musik* IV, no. 29 (April 8, 1836), 123.

[36]See Macdonald, "The Genesis of Schumann's Phantasie," 255.

[37]Hermann Erler, *Robert Schumann's Leben: Aus seinen Briefen*, vol. 1 (Berlin: Verlag von Ries & Erler, 1887), 261.

[38]Jon William Finson, *Robert Schumann: The Creation of the Symphonic Works* (Ph.D. diss., The University of Chicago, 1980), 22.

[39]Julius Eckardt, *Ferdinand David und die Familie Mendelssohn-Bartholdy* (Leipzig: Duncker & Humblot, 1888), 150–51.

[40]Werner Schwarz, "Eine Musikerfreundschaft des 19. Jahrhunderts. Unveröffentlichte Briefe von Ferdinand David an Robert Schumann," in *Zum 70. Geburstag von Joseph Müller-Blattau* (Kassel; Bärenreiter, 1966), 285–6.

[41]*Tagebücher*, 2:179 (July 18 to August 8).

[42]Siegfried Kross, ed., *Briefe und Notizen Robert und Clara Schumanns* (Bonn: Bouvier Verlag Herbert Grundman, 1982), 199 (August 9, 1841).

[43]*Haushaltbücher*, 190.

[44]*Tagebücher*, 2:180–81.

[45]Archive of the Robert-Schumann-Haus (Zwickau), no. 8847—A2 (undated).

[46]*Tagebücher*, 2:183.

[47]In a letter of October 6, 1843 to Carl Gotthelf Böhme (of C. F. Peters in Leipzig), Schumann described the fantasy as "*Allegro affettuoso* for pianoforte with orchestral accompaniment, Op. 48." Archive of the Heinrich-Heine-Institut (Düsseldorf), acquisition no. 1 83.5029. (The Op. 48 now belongs to the song cycle *Dichterliebe*.)

[48]Bernhard R. Appel, "Die Überleitung vom 2. zum 3. Satz in Robert Schumanns Klavierkonzert Opus 54," *Die Musikforschung* 44 (1991), 260.

[49]Archive of the Robert-Schumann-Haus (Zwickau), no. 7236—A2 (January 23, 1843).

[50]*Haushaltbücher*, 235.

[51]Victor Joss, *Der Musikpädagoge Friedrich Wieck und seine Familie. Mit besonderer Berücksichtigung seines Schwiegersohnes Robert Schumann.* (Dresden: Verlag von Oscar Damm, 1902), 83.

[52]*Haushaltbücher*, 237 (February 9, 1843).

[53]Archive of the Heinrich-Heine-Institut (Düsseldorf), acquisition no. 83.5029 (October 6, 1843).

[54]*Briefe: Neue Folge*, 438.

[55]*Haushaltbücher*, 391.

[56]Ibid., 393–4.

[57]Berthold Litzmann, *Clara Schumann: Ein Künstlerleben. Nach Tagebüchern und Briefen*, vol. 2 (*"Ehejahre" 1840–56*), 2nd ed. (Leipzig: Breitkopf & Härtel, 1906), 133.

[58]*Haushaltbücher*, 394.

[59]Ibid., 395.

[60]Ibid., 396.

[61]Stephen Roe, "The Autograph Manuscript of Schumann's Piano Concerto," *The Musical Times* 131 (1990), 77.

[62]Litzmann, 2:133.

[63]*Haushaltbücher*, 395.

[64]Litzmann, 2:138.

[65]*Haushaltbücher*, 399.

[66]Ibid., 407.

[67]Reinhold Sietz, *Aus Ferdinand Hillers Briefwechsel (1826–61)*, Beiträge zur Rheinischen Musikgeschichte 28 (Cologne: Arno Volk-Verlag, 1958), 59 (undated).

[68]*Haushaltbücher*, 407.

[69]*Allgemeine Musikalische Zeitung* 52 (December 31, 1845), 928.

[70]Karl Laux, "Dresden ist doch gar zu schön. Schumann in der Sächsischen Haupstadt. Eine Ehrenrettung," in *Robert Schumann. Aus Anlass seines 100. Todestages*, ed. Hans Joachim Moser and Eberhard Rebling (Leipzig: Breitkopf & Härtel, 1956), 29 (December 25, 1845).

[71]"Aus Dresden. Concerte," *Neue Zeitschrift für Musik* XXIV, no. 9 (January 29, 1846), 35–36.

[72]"Für Pianoforte," ibid., XXVI, no. 5 (January 15, 1847), 17.

[73]*Briefe: Neue Folge*, 254 (erroneously dated November 12, 1845). See Robert Schumann, *Briefverzeichnis, Abgesandte Briefe* (no. 900). Archive of the Robert-Schumann-Haus (Zwickau), no. 4871/VII C/10—A3 (December 12, 1845).

[74]Ibid., 255 (erroneously dated November 18, 1845). See Robert Schumann, *Briefverzeichnis, Abgesandte Briefe* (no. 1142). Archive of the Robert-Schumann-Haus (Zwickau), no. 4871/VII C/10—A3.

[75]Nancy B. Reich, "The Correspondence between Clara Wieck-Schumann and Felix and Paul Mendelssohn," in *Schumann and his World*, ed. R. Larry Todd (Princeton: Princeton University Press, 1994), 222.

[76]*Briefe: Neue Folge*, 518 (note 314).

[77]Erler, *Robert Schumann's Leben*, 2:1 (January 2, 1846).

[78]*Haushaltbücher*, 411.

[79]Ibid., 673.

[80]Litzmann, 2:273.

[81]*Briefe: Neue Folge*, 399 (September 18, 1854).

[82]Eduard Hanslick, *Aus dem Concert-Saal. Kritiken und Schilderungen aus 20 Jahren des Wiener Musiklebens 1848–68*, 2nd ed. (Vienna: Wilhelm Braumüller, 1897), 183.

[83]*Briefe: Neue Folge*, 255 (December 18, 1845).

[84]See Appel, "Die Überleitung," 255–61.

[85] Meaning "empty," the syllables *Vi-* and *–de* were often used to indicate an optional omission in a score, or in this instance to direct the performer to proceed directly from that marked *Vi-* to that marked *–de*.

[86] Robert Schumann, *Gesammelte Schriften über Musik und Musiker*, 5th ed., ed. Martin Kreisig, vol. 2 (Leipzig: Breitkopf & Härtel, 1914), 117.

[87] Arnfried Edler, *Robert Schumann und seine Zeit* (N.p.: Laaber-Verlag, 1982), 159 ff.

[88] Short for "Soggetto cavato dalle parole" (literally "subject carved out of the words"), a term first used by the 16th-century music theorist Gioseffo Zarlino for the practice of creating a musical subject from the corresponding letters of a word.

[89] Robert Schumann, *Konzert für Klavier und Orchester a-Moll, Op. 54. Taschenpartitur, Einführung und Analyse*, ed. Egon Voss (Mainz: B. Schott's Söhne, 1979), 215.

[90] "Das Clavier-Concert," *Neue Zeitschrift für Musik* X, no. 2 (January 4, 1839), 6.

[91] Berthold Litzmann, *Clara Schumann: Ein Künstlerleben. Nach Tagebüchern und Briefen*, vol. 3 ("*Clara Schumann und ihre Freunde*" 1856–1896), 2nd ed. (Leipzig: Breitkopf & Härtel, 1906), 619.

[92] *Projektenbuch* ("Compositionsübersicht"), 51.

[93] Hanslick, *Aus dem Concert-Saal*, 182.

[94] Archive of the Robert-Schumann-Haus (Zwickau), no. 4501, Bd. 2.

[95] Gustav Jansen, *Die Davidsbündler: Aus Robert Schumann's Sturm- und Drangperiode* (Leipzig: Breitkopf & Härtel, 1883; reprint, Wiesbaden: Dr. Martin Sändig oHG, 1973), 74.

[96] *Brockhaus Riemann Musiklexikon*, ed. Carl Dahlhaus and Hans Heinrich Eggebrecht, vol. 3 (Mainz: B. Schott's Söhne, 1989), 283.

[97] *Briefe: Neue Folge*, 365 (February 8, 1853).

[98] See Dietrich Kämper, "Zur Frage der Metronombezeichnungen Robert Schumanns," *Archiv für Musikwissenschaft* 31 (August 1964): 141–55; and Brian Schlotel, "Schumann and the Metronome," in *Robert Schumann. The Man and his Music*, ed. Alan Walker (New York: Barnes and Noble, 1974): 109–19.

[99] Payment for Mehner's services (six Thalers and twenty Neugroschen) was recorded by Schumann in the household book, *Haushaltbücher*, 399 (September 1, 1845).

[100] *Robert Schumanns Briefe: Neue Folge*, ed. F. Gustav Jansen, 2nd ed. (Leipzig: Breitkopf & Härtel, 1904), 445.

[101] Archive of the Robert-Schumann-Haus (Zwickau), no. 4509, Bd. 9, A3.

[102] Kurt Hofmann, *Die Erstdrucke der Werke von Robert Schumann* (Tutzing: Hans Schneider, 1979), 123.

[103] *Klavierwerke von Robert Schumann. Erste mit Fingersatz und Vortragsbezeichnung versehene Instructive Ausgabe. Nach den Handschriften und persönlicher Überlieferung.*

[104] Hans von Bülow, *Ausgewählte Schriften: 1850–92* (Leipzig: Breitkopf & Härtel, 1896), 132.